Marmalade
and the
Magic Birds

To
Elizabeth
and
Rufus

Barefoot Books
37 West 17th Street
4th Floor East
New York, NY 10011

This book was typeset in Comic Sans
Illustration medium: Taking some red, yellow and blue, Robin stirred them up in his Apple Mac
computer using Painter 6. He then cooked them in Photoshop 5 until they tasted just right

Graphic design by Design Principals, Warminster, England
Color separation by Color Gallery, Malaysia
Printed and bound in Hong Kong by South China Printing Co (1988) Ltd

This book has been printed on 100% acid-free paper

ISBN 1 84148 316 8

1 3 5 7 9 8 6 4 2

U.S. Cataloging-in-Publication Data (Library of Congress Standards)

Harris, Robin.
    Marmalade and the magic birds / written and illustrated
by Robin Harris.
[32] p. : col. ill. ; 28 cm.
Summary: When a magician steals the birds from Marmalade's
backyard, the clever cat knows he must get them back.
ISBN: 1-84148-316-8
1.Cats -- Fiction. 2. Magic tricks -- Fiction. I. Title.
[E] 21 2001   AC   CIP

Marmalade and the Magic Birds

Written and illustrated
by Robin Harris

Marmalade was painting his house
while the birds sang in his garden.
Suddenly, he heard an alarming noise:
"Twitter, tweet, squawk, SQUAWK!"
"Oh no!" thought Marmalade.
"Someone is stealing the birds!"

He raced out of the house and
sprang over the garden fence,
shouting, "Stop, thief!"

"You won't stop me that easily!"
retorted the tall stranger.

"I am Ertax the Tanfastic, and I can do whatever I like!"

Then he boomed out:

"OM-POM-PUSH!"

Marmalade stopped and scratched his chin.

"Where's he gone? He was here a moment ago."

The magician's voice boomed out again:

"I am Ertax the Tanfastic and I can do whatever I like! OM-POM-PUSH!"

"I know you're in here somewhere," muttered Marmalade, rummaging through an old car. "I can hear you."

"Ha ha ha!" chuckled Ertax the Tanfastic. "You may be able to hear me, but can you see me? OM-POM-PUSH!"

"Let go of those birds, wherever you are!" shouted Marmalade. "They should be free. You can't just steal them."

"Of course I can!" the magician replied. "I am Ertax the
Tanfastic, and I can do whatever I like. OM-POM-PUSH!"
"There you are," cried Marmalade. "Let those birds go!"

"Not on your life," said Ertax the Tanfastic.
"I need them for something very special."
And he turned back into a normal magician and
headed straight for the theater.

Marmalade crept quietly
after him and watched.

Ertax the Tanfastic waved
his magic wand.

Marmalade gazed in wonder
as all the birds flew out of
the magician's hat.

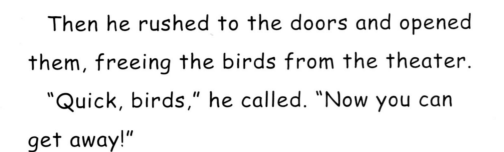

Then he rushed to the doors and opened them, freeing the birds from the theater.

"Quick, birds," he called. "Now you can get away!"

The grateful birds swooped through the open doors and flew up to the sky.

Marmalade turned to face the magician. "You should not keep birds cooped up in your hat," he said sternly.

"I'm sorry, I'm sorry," sobbed Ertax the Tanfastic. "But there can be no magic show without birds, and mine are all sick."

"Are your tears real or just magic?" asked Marmalade.

"Real," sobbed the magician.

"Then come with me," said Marmalade. "I have an idea."

"Why are we buying all these toy
airplanes?" asked Ertax the Tanfastic.
"Wait and see," replied Marmalade.

As he watched his new friend paint the airplanes, Ertax the Tanfastic smiled.

"Can I be your assistant?" asked Marmalade.

"You can!" replied Ertax the Tanfastic.

OM-POM-PUSH!

All the children clapped and cheered as the painted paper planes flew from Ertax the Tanfastic's wonderful hat.

After the show, each child took home a painted airplane.

Above them, the birds swooped and sang.

"And now," said Marmalade, "it's time for us to go home too, and have a nice cup of tea with the birds."

Barefoot Books
better books for children
www.barefootbooks.com

At Barefoot Books, we celebrate art and story with books that open
the hearts and minds of children from all walks of life, inspiring them to read
deeper, search further, and explore their own creative gifts. Taking our
inspiration from many different cultures, we focus on themes that encourage
independence of spirit, enthusiasm for learning, and acceptance of other
traditions. Thoughtfully prepared by writers, artists and storytellers from
all over the world, our products combine the best of the present with the best
of the past to educate our children as the caretakers of tomorrow.
www.barefootbooks.com